o be fit:
way
lay

Don't Be A Schwoe
FITNESS
Schiffer Publishing Ltd
4880 Lower Valley Road • Atglen, PA 19310
Written by Barbara E. Mauzy
Illustrated by Bob Stuhmer

Beyond the oceans and over the bay,
There is a land so far, far away
That we can't reach it for many a day.

I have not been there, but I have heard
To find this place you follow a bird
That first flies north and then turns eastward.

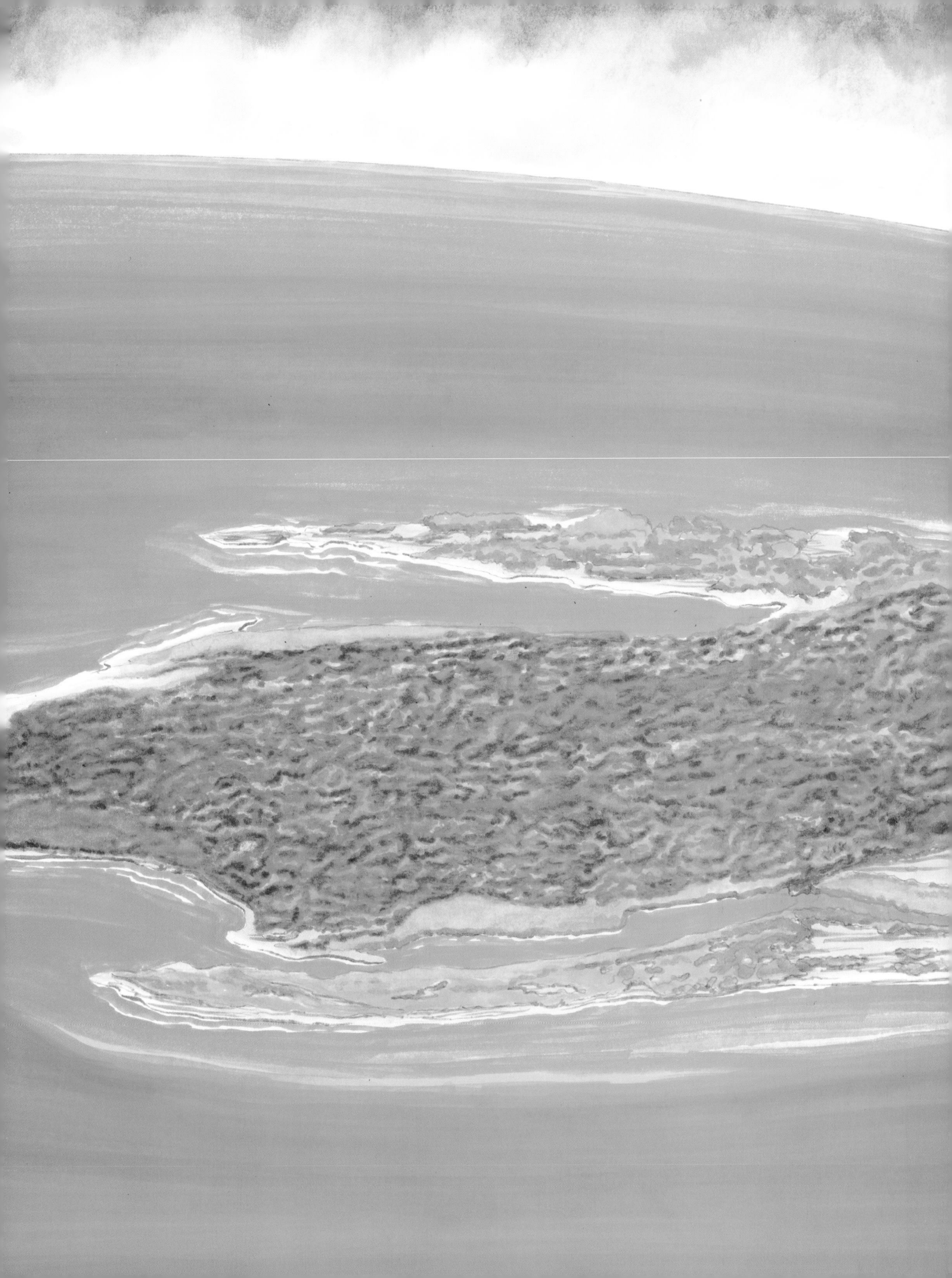

When you come to the narrow crook
Along the stream called "Sunfish Brook"
Climb any tree and take a look.

You've almost reached that strange place
Far from the bustling human race.
It's time to pack your best suitcase.

Together you and I will go
To find the land of Par-zee-no,
Home of the mysterious Schwoe.

WELCOME
TO
PAR-ZEE-NO
HOME OF THE MYSTERIOUS SCHWOE

They're usually purple, don't you know.
That's how it is, if you're a Schwoe.
(One is red and fuzzy though.)

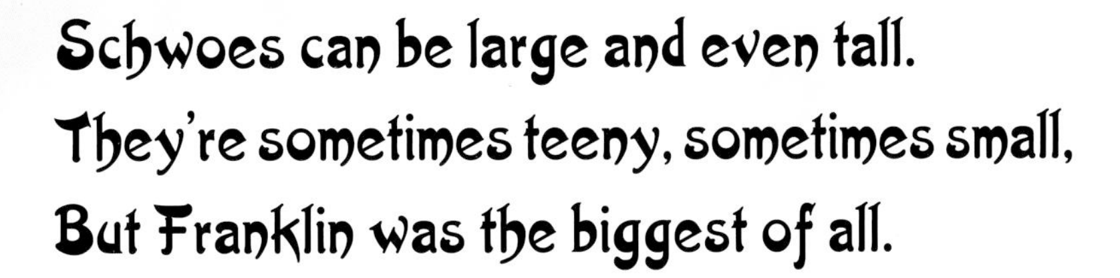

Schwoes can be large and even tall.
They're sometimes teeny, sometimes small,
But Franklin was the biggest of all.

Franklin was a chubby, young Schwoe
With several chins that hung real low.
Why this was, he did not know.

The concerned Schwoes of Par-zee-no
Worried as they watched Franklin grow
A tummy like bowls of grape Jell-o.

He did little more than munch, munch, munch.
From breakfast until noontime lunch,
They listened for his crunchy crunch.

After lunch Franklin rested a bit.

Then to the table he returned to sit
And eat some more; he didn't quit.

Franklin's Schwoe Mommy was really quite sad.
Which also was true of his loving Schwoe Dad.

Franklin had grown into a huge Schwoe lad.

Mommy thought Franklin needed to stop.

Dad thought exercise – run, skip, hop –

Would help round Franklin's weight to drop.

Franklin didn't agree at all,
And gobbled a peach, pit and all.
He'd rather eat than kick a ball.

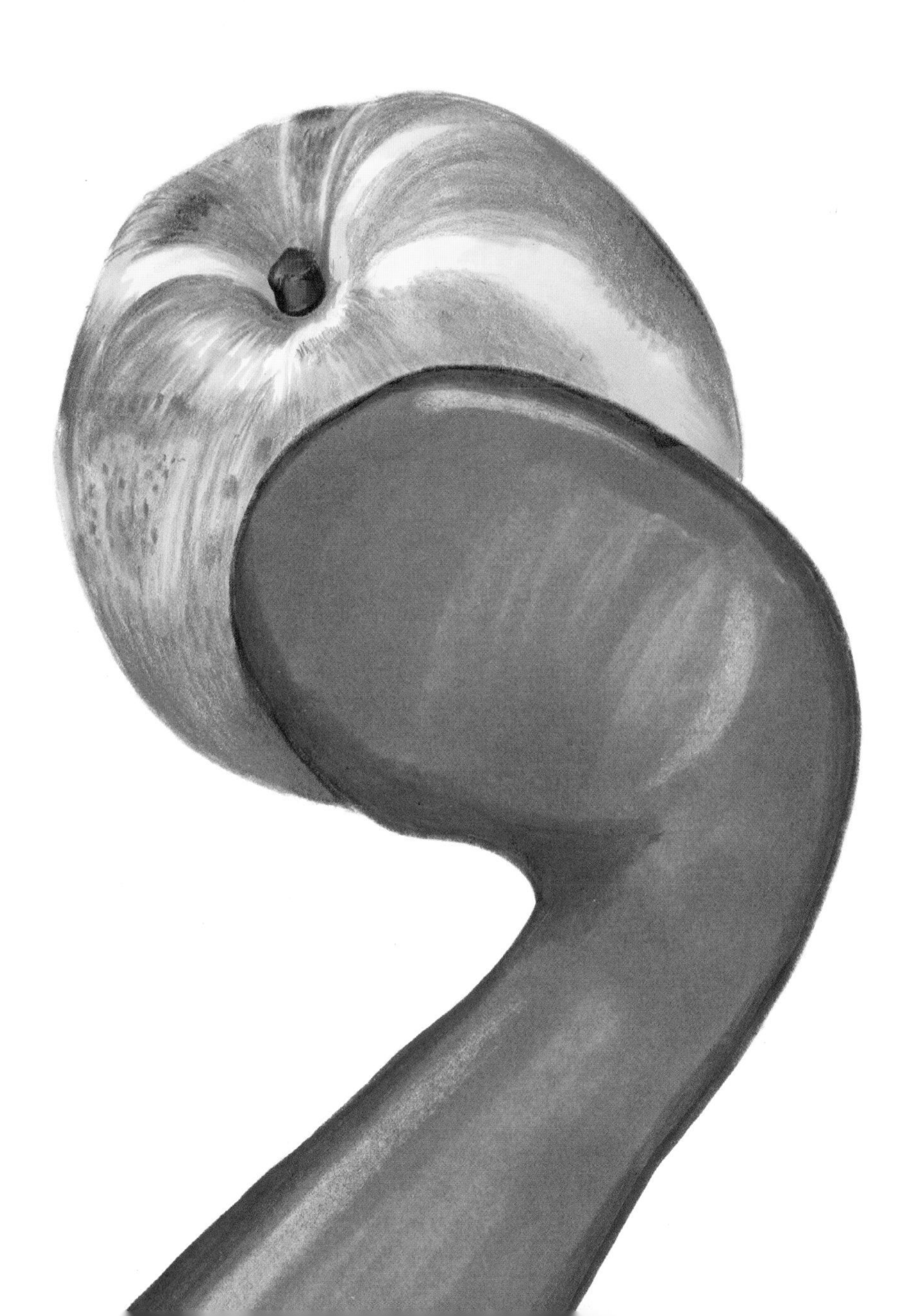

To help Franklin lose his
excess weight
Before it was harder or
simply too late,
With the doctor Schwoe
Mommy made a date.

OFFICE OF
DOCTOR SCHWOE

The doctor examined Franklin Schwoe
To determine which was the best way to go,
And then let Franklin and his parents know.

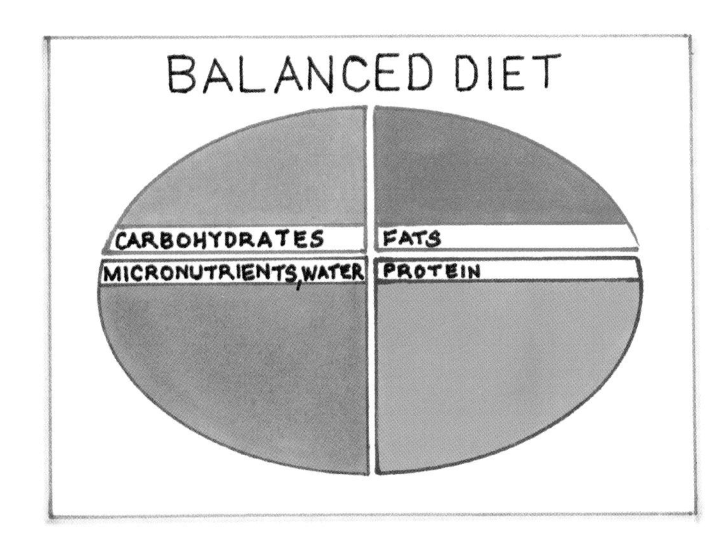

"It's not that hard; it's really so easy,"
The doctor told Franklin, who was
feeling quite queasy.
"Soon you'll be fit and light and feel
breezy!"

"It's as simple as this! Eat less at each meal
And exercise more. It'll help how you feel.
Franklin, my boy, let's make a deal."

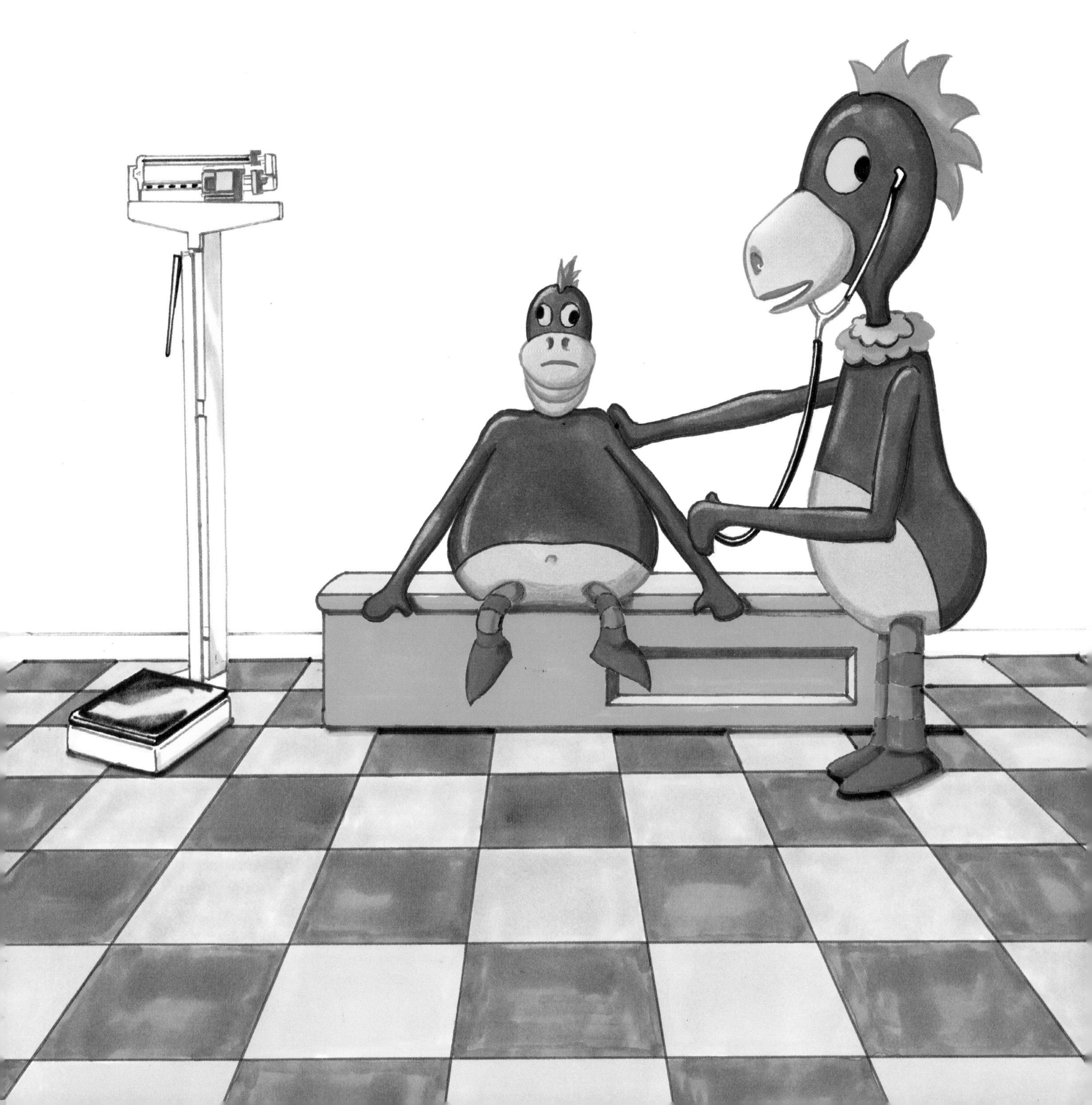

The doctor leaned close to the young, round Schwoe
Who had all those pounds that needed to go,
And then whispered something...
what I don't know.

But Franklin broke out in a huge grinny grin
That jiggled each one of his three
chinny chins.
"Okay, doc," he agreed,
"Let's begin!"

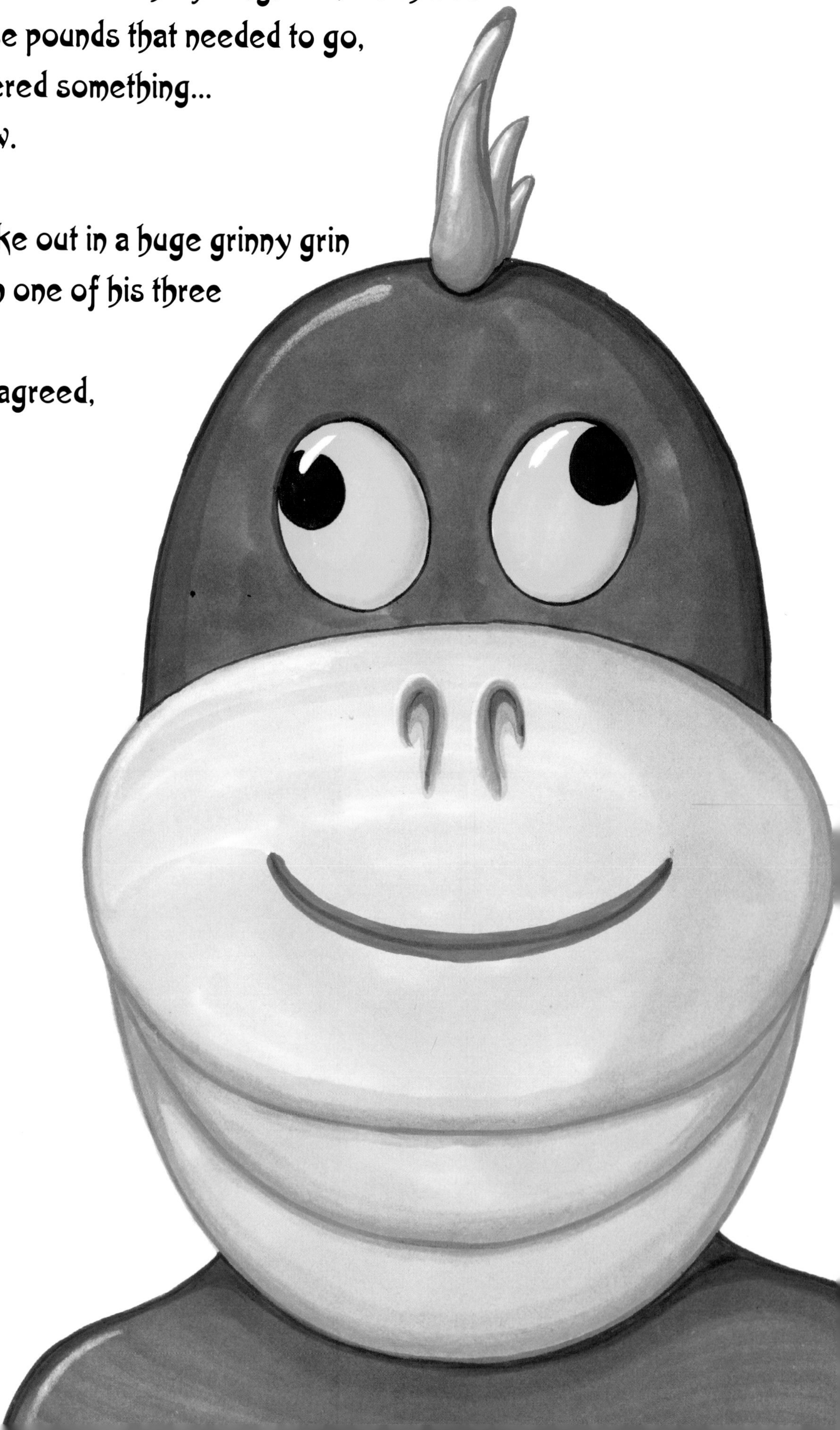

He went home with a brand new resolve:
A new, fit Franklin soon would evolve
If he could make some weight dissolve.

He found his sneakers and went outside.
"Yes, common sense must be my guide,
But at least I'll know that I tried."

The chubby Schwoe said quietly,
"I can do this! Watch, wait, and see!"
And he took a walk, most happily.

And so it was that, day after day,
Franklin Schwoe changed in little ways,
Eating less and learning to play.

He made new friends, that Franklin did!
Picking teams? He no longer hid.
All those pounds he started to rid.

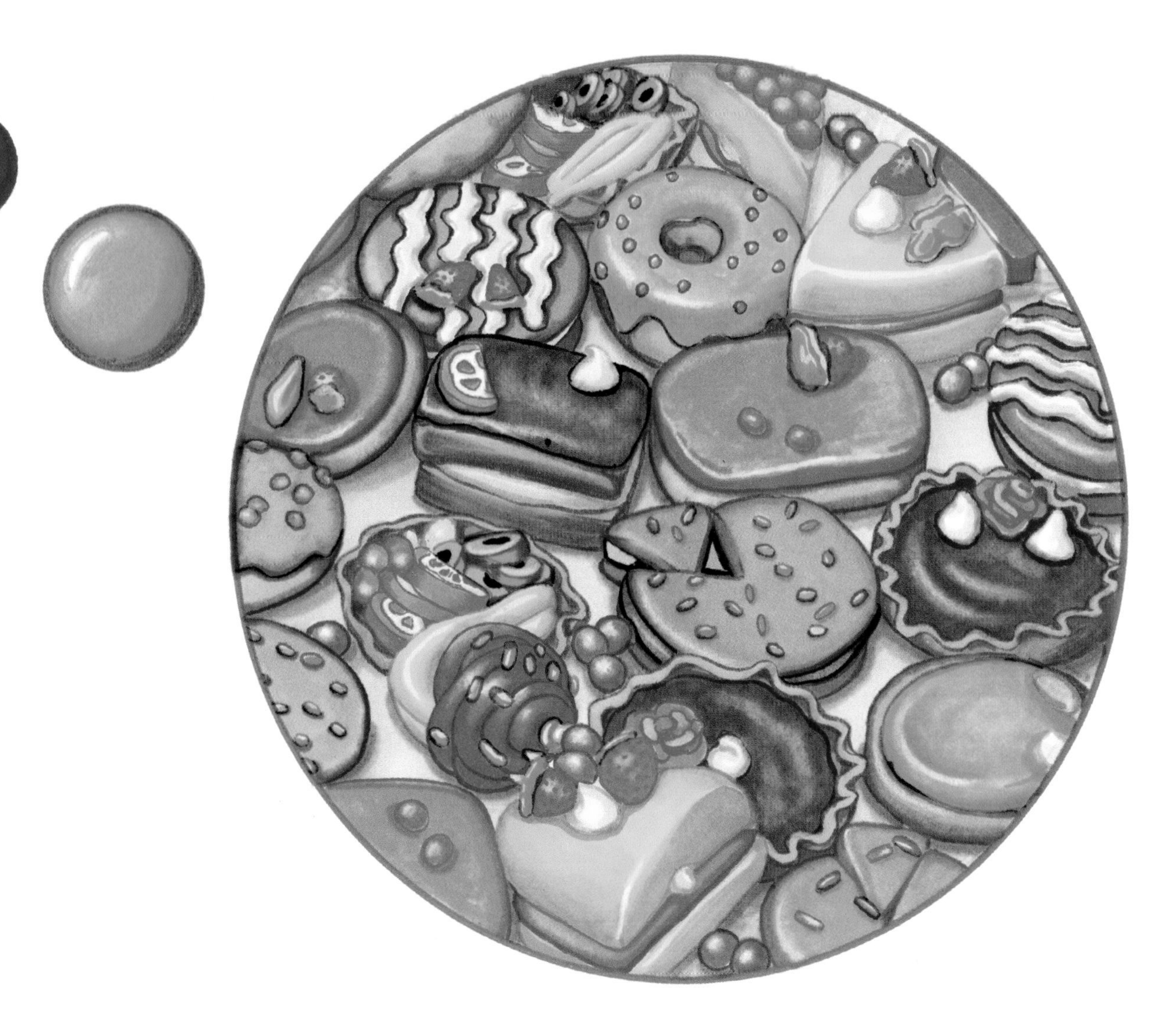

Oh, there were days that were rough and tough,
When salads and fruits were not quite enough.
He wanted only sugary stuff.

Sometimes he grumped,
sometimes he cried,

And there were
days when
he moped and
sighed.

But overall Franklin
really tried.

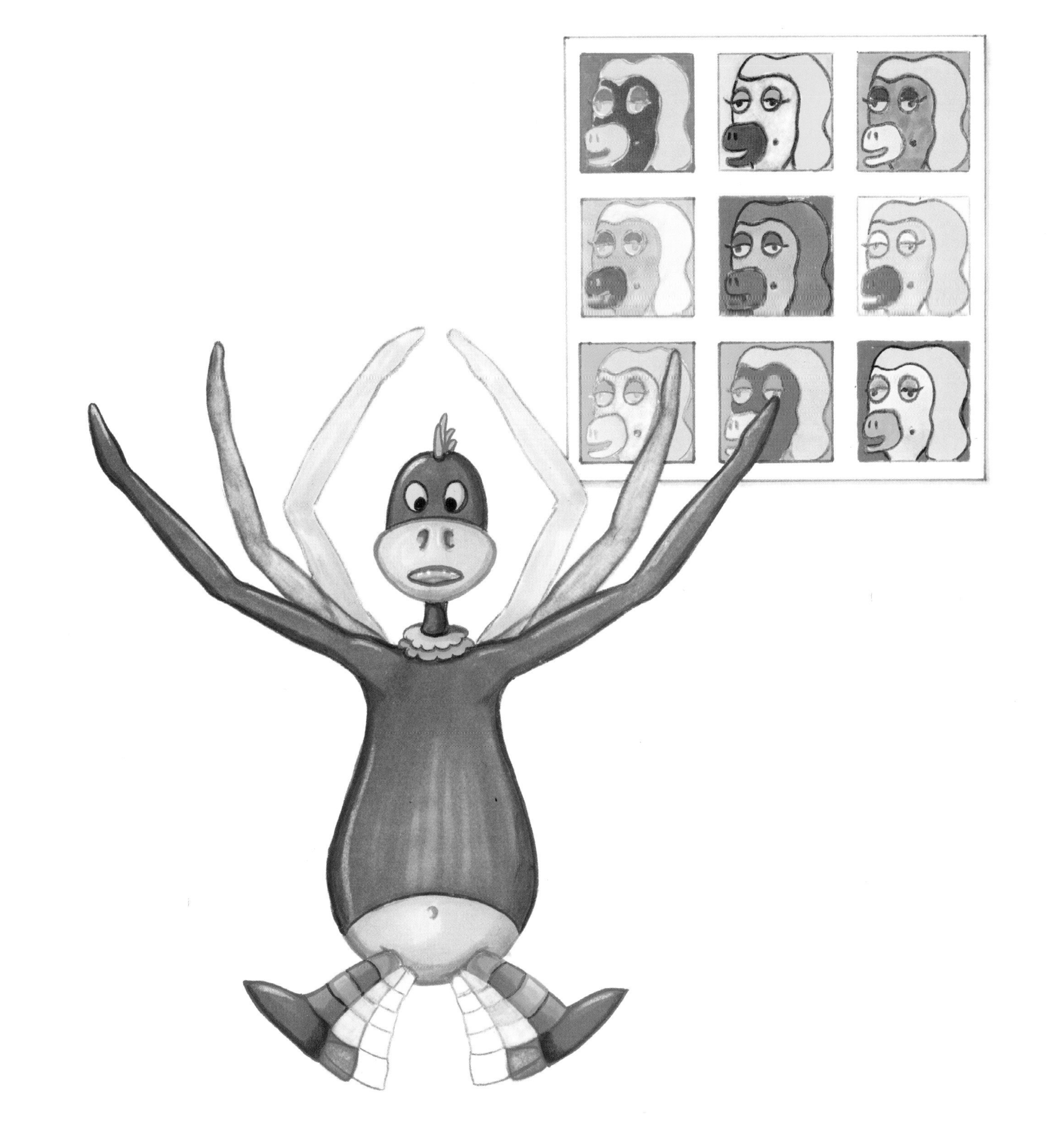

And time went on, day after day.
You know it does, it has its way.
And through it all, Franklin was okay.

When six months had passed our little Franklin,

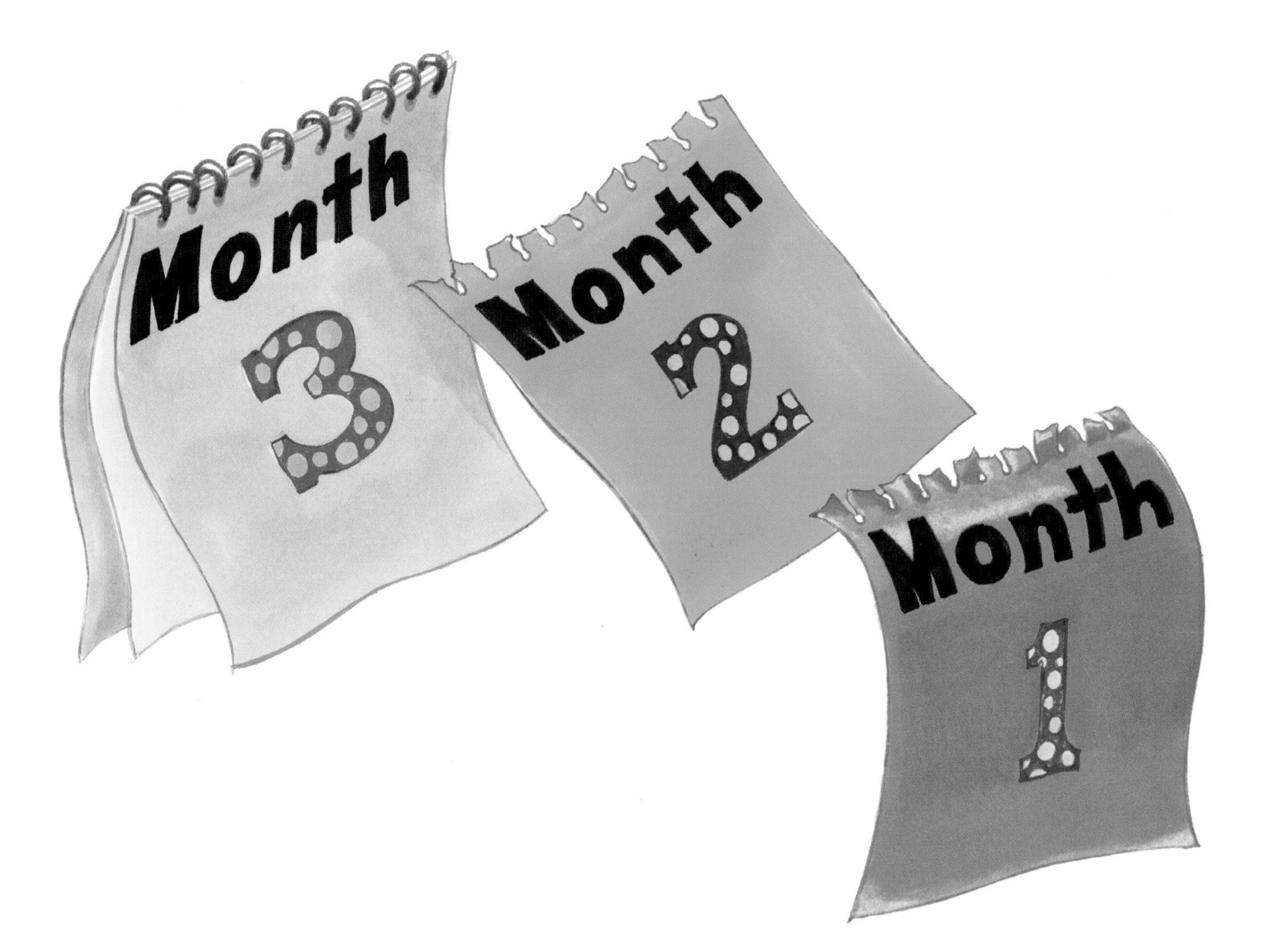

Went to Doc Schwoe with a very broad grin
That showed he had only one chinny chin.

Onto the scales climbed the Franklin lad
And applause rose up from Mom and Dad.
"*Really* great results! We're so glad!"

Franklin had changed in many new ways:
Eating good foods, wanting to play.
Proudly Franklin shouted out, "Yea!"

Doctor Schwoe smiled and cleared his throat,
"Franklin, I know you want to gloat,
But we made a deal. Here's your boat."

To the smaller, healthier Schwoe
The doc gave a box wrapped up with a bow.
Franklin said, "Thanks. But I've got to go!"

He skipped outside with a fast "Goodbye,"
And seeing some friends, he shouted, "Hi!
Let's play with my boat! We all can try!"

The Schwoes quickly
hiked to Sunfish Brook,
And one by one their
turns they took
With Franklin, his boat,
and his brand new look.

What to remember to be fit:
1. Eat in a healthy way
2. Exercise every day

As time passed and Franklin
Schwoe grew
There was one thing he
always knew.
Well, actually there were *two:*

Always eat in a healthy way.
Take time to exercise each day.
That's how a Schwoe
(and you) can stay…

Looking good, even feeling fit,
Not overweight a single bit!
Move around. Don't just sit,
sit, sit!

It worked great for a
chubby Schwoe.
It makes extra pounds
simply go, go, go.
It's the same for YOU!
Now YOU know!

Other Schiffer Books by the Author:

Don't be a Schwoe: Embracing Differences. 978-0-7643-3566-2, $16.99
Don't be a Schwoe: Manners. 978-0-7643-3428-3, $14.99

Library of Congress Control Number: 2012956312

Designed by Danielle D. Farmer
Type set in Artistik

ISBN: 978-0-7643-4295-0
Printed in China

Published by Schiffer Publishing, Ltd.
4880 Lower Valley Road
Atglen, PA 19310
Phone: (610) 593-1777; Fax: (610) 593-2002
E-mail: Info@schifferbooks.com

In Europe, Schiffer books are distributed by
Bushwood Books
6 Marksbury Ave.
Kew Gardens
Surrey TW9 4JF England
Phone: 44 (0) 20 8392 8585; Fax: 44 (0) 20 8392 9876
E-mail: info@bushwoodbooks.co.uk
Website: www.bushwoodbooks.co.uk